This book belongs to:

....

Based on the episode "Paddington and the Dinosaur Hunt" by Jon Foster and James Lamont

Adapted by Lauren Holowaty

First published in the United Kingdom by HarperCollins *Children's Books* in 2024
HarperCollins *Children's Books* is a division of HarperCollins*Publishers* Ltd
1 London Bridge Street
London SE1 9GF

www.harpercollins.co.uk

HarperCollins*Publishers*
Macken House, 39/40 Mayor Street Upper
Dublin 1, D01 C9W8, Ireland

2 3 5 7 9 10 8 6 4

ISBN: 978-0-00-864426-0

Printed in the United Kingdom

Conditions of Sale

Based on the Paddington novels written and created by Michael Bond

This book is produced from independently certified FSC™ paper
to ensure responsible forest management.

For more information visit: www.harpercollins.co.uk/green

The Adventures of Paddington™

The Dinosaur Hunt

HarperCollins *Children's Books*

Dear Aunt Lucy,

My special dinosaur book finally arrived in the post. I'd been waiting for it for ages, and all I wanted to do was read it . . .

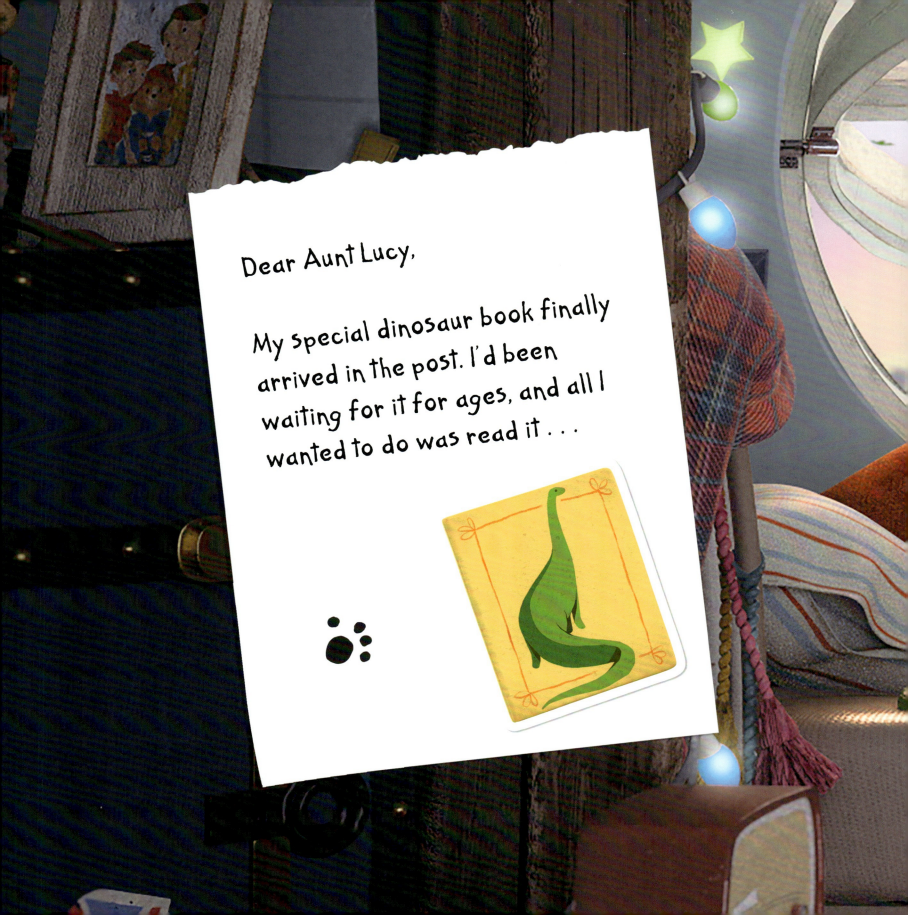

One morning, a **special parcel** arrived for Paddington in the post.

"It's here, everyone!" Paddington announced, holding up his new dinosaur book. But the kitchen was empty. "Oh . . . They must all still be in bed."

Paddington sat down to read his new book.

"It's amazing that millions of years ago, dinosaurs roamed the Earth. Some probably lived right here in Windsor Gardens . . ." he said out loud, when suddenly he heard a terrifying noise!

RAAGGGGHHHHH!

Mr Brown walked into the kitchen, yawning so loudly Paddington thought he was a roaring dinosaur!

"MY GOODNESS!" gasped Paddington.

"Morning, Paddington," said Mr Brown.

"Morning, Mr Brown. I thought you were a dinosau—AHHH!" cried Paddington as a T-rex **sprang up** from his book.

"I'm not *that* old, Paddington!" said Mr Brown.

Paddington poked his head up from under the table. "So, it's definitely not a real dinosaur?"

"It's just a pop-up one, Paddington," said Mr Brown. "Dinosaurs are extinct."

Jonathan raced in. "Want to come to the park, Paddington? Simi and I are off to explore No-man's Island!"

"How exciting!" replied Paddington.

"It's for a school science project and there's a prize for the best work," explained Jonathan.

"Well, I *was* reading my new book . . ." said Paddington. "But dinosaurs can wait."

Paddington had never explored No-man's Island before. He didn't know *who* or *what* was living there. But he was curious to find out!

"Please could you give us a ride to the island, Mr Curry?" asked Jonathan.

"I'm extremely busy," said Mr Curry, feeding the ducks. "Well, okay, just this once."

Mr Curry took the brave explorers to No-man's Island in a boat.
"I'll meet you back here when the sun sets," he said, then motored off.

To win the science prize, the explorers needed to find wildlife. So, they trudged along the shore in search of it.

SQUELCH! SQUELCH!

It was so muddy that poor Paddington sank. "Jonathan! Simi!" he called. "I seem to be **rather stuck!**"

Just then Paddington noticed something in the mud.

"Footprints!" announced Jonathan. "Something *is* living here."

The footprints had three toes.

"My book says some **dinosaurs** only had three toes," said Paddington.

"No-man's Island could be the **last place in the world where** dinosaurs *still live*!" said Simi. "Let's follow the footprints!"

Suddenly something fluttery landed on Paddington's nose. "Help! I appear to have grown whiskers!"

"It's a dragonfly," said Simi. "An ancient creature, just like the dinosaur." She pointed to some plants. "These were around in dinosaur times too."

"Everything on this island is rather *dinosaury*," said Paddington, "just like in my book."

As the dragonfly flew off, Jonathan followed it and stumbled upon something very exciting.

"Quick! Over here!" he called.

"Oooh! A dinosaur eggshell," said Simi. "Perhaps a dinosaur only just hatched?"

Paddington picked up the shell and imagined a dinky dinosaur hatching out of the egg.

"So – it must be small then?" he asked hopefully.

"No, whatever it is will be **bigger** by now!" said Simi.

Paddington imagined a HUGE
dinosaur holding *him* instead . . .

ROAAAARRR!

"ARGGGHHH!"

"My book says that dinosaurs are either carnivores, which means meat-eaters, or herbivores, which means plant-eaters," said Paddington, as they continued their search.

"I hope it's a **carnivore!**" said Jonathan.

"I hope it's a **herbivore!**" said Paddington.

"**Look! A feather,**" shouted Simi. "It could belong to a dinosaur. Some experts think dinosaurs had feathers."

Paddington imagined the HUGE dinosaur now *also* had feathers.

"**ARGGGHHH!**" he cried, terrified at the thought.

The explorers had been tracking the dinosaur all day, but they still hadn't found it. The sun was just beginning to set when there was a terrifying sound . . .

GWACK, ACK, ACK!

"It's coming this way!" Jonathan whispered.

Just then, a bird flew out of the bushes.

"Oh, thank goodness! It's just a goose," sighed Paddington.

"The egg must have been hers!" realised Simi. "She must be protecting her babies."

GWAAACCCCKKKK!

The angry goose started to chase Paddington.

She followed them round and round the island until they climbed up a tree to hide.

"Phew! I think we lost her," said Simi.

From up high, Paddington spotted Mr Curry approaching. The explorers silently slid down the tree and raced to his boat as quietly as they could.

But the goose heard and raced out of the bushes after them . . .

GWAAACCCCKKKK!

Jonathan and Simi leaped into the boat, but Paddington couldn't run as fast! The goose was getting closer and closer!

"Quick! Start the engine!" shouted Jonathan. But the engine wouldn't work.

"Hurry, Mr Curry!" gasped Paddington, jumping into the boat and throwing on a life jacket. They watched the goose dash down the jetty, frantically flapping its wings.

"Distract her!" shouted Simi.

Paddington spotted Mr Curry's **birdseed** and quickly tipped it out on to the jetty.

The goose stopped to peck the seed, and everyone sighed in relief. "PHEW!"

"So, the island *was* inhabited after all," said Jonathan, taking pictures. "Just *not* by a dinosaur."

The little goslings waddled down to join their mum.

"In my book it says that birds are the descendants of dinosaurs," said Paddington.

"So . . . we *did* find a dinosaur . . . kind of!" said Simi.

In the end, Aunt Lucy, Jonathan won the science prize and we all shared it. He was allowed to choose his prize and decided upon an explorer's kit! And I was sure there were no dinosaurs roaming Windsor Gardens after all. Probably . . .

Love from,
Paddington